T0310510

# Katy Duck

and the
## Tip-Top Tap Shoes

By Alyssa Satin Capucilli  Illustrated by Henry Cole

Ready-to-Read

Simon Spotlight

New York   London   Toronto   Sydney   New Delhi

For my most tip-top editor, Valerie, with love!
—A. S. C.

SIMON SPOTLIGHT
An imprint of Simon & Schuster Children's Publishing Division
1230 Avenue of the Americas, New York, New York 10020
Text copyright © 2013 by Alyssa Satin Capucilli
Illustrations copyright © 2013 by Henry Cole
All rights reserved, including the right of reproduction in whole or in part in any form.
SIMON SPOTLIGHT, READY-TO-READ, and colophon are registered trademarks of
Simon & Schuster, Inc.
For information about special discounts for bulk purchases, please contact Simon & Schuster
Special Sales at 1-866-506-1949 or business@simonandschuster.com.
The Simon & Schuster Speakers Bureau can bring authors to your live event. For more information or
to book an event contact the Simon & Schuster Speakers Bureau at 1-866-248-3049 or visit our website
at www.simonspeakers.com.
Manufactured in the United States of America 0422 LAK
10 9 8 7 6 5 4 3
Library of Congress Cataloging-in-Publication Data
Capucilli, Alyssa Satin, 1957-
Katy Duck and the tip-top tap shoes / by Alyssa Satin Capucilli ; illustrated by Henry Cole. — 1st ed.
p. cm. — (Ready-to-read)
Summary: When the new student in Katy Duck's ballet class makes a tapping sound, the music stops
and everyone looks at her feet.
ISBN 978-1-4424-5246-6 (hardcover) — ISBN 978-1-4424-5245-9 (pbk.) — ISBN 978-1-4424-5247-3
(ebook)
[1. Ballet —Fiction. 2. Tap dancing —Fiction. 3. Dance —Fiction. 4. Ducks —Fiction.] I. Cole, Henry,
1955- ill. II. Title.
PZ7.C179Kag 2013
[E] —dc23
2011052608

There was a new duck
in dance class.
Katy Duck wanted
to meet her!

"Tra-la-la. Quack! Quack!
My name is Katy Duck.
I love to dance."

"Tra-la-la. Tap! Tap!
My name is Alice Duck.
I love to dance too."

The music began.

Katy felt her arms flutter.

Her feet began to

pitter-patter.

# Tip-top-tap!
# Tip-top-tap!
## What was that sound?

**Tap! Tap! Tap!**

It was Alice Duck!

Alice Duck had tap shoes.

The tap shoes were black.

They were very shiny.

They made tapping sounds!

**Tap! Tap! Tap!**

"Stop the music," called
Mr. Tutu.
"Stop the music,
please!"

"Now, now, " said Mr. Tutu.
"You do not need tap
shoes in here, Alice.
This is ballet class."

"Tra-la-la. Tap! Tap!
But I love my tap shoes,"
said Alice.

Alice tapped
here.

Alice tapped
there.

"My tap shoes are tip-top!"

Mr. Tutu rubbed his chin.

The class grew quiet.

Katy Duck looked right.

She looked left.

"Wait!" said Katy Duck.
"I have an idea.
You can try my extra
slippers!"

"You can float
like a swan.
And sway like a flower.

You can wear your
tip-top tap shoes
after ballet class."

Alice looked down at her
shiny tap shoes.
She looked at Katy's
soft slippers.

"That sounds like a
tip-top idea to me!"
said Alice Duck.

Alice and Katy stretched
high. They bent low.

After class,
Alice asked Katy,
"Would you like to
try my tap shoes?"

"Oh yes!" said Katy.

**Tip-top-tap!**

**Tip-top-tap!**

"Tap shoes are fun!"

Alice swayed. She floated.
"Ballet slippers are fun
too," said Alice Duck.

"Tra-la-la. Tap! Tap!
Tra-la-la. Quack! Quack!
How we **love** to dance!"